She'd fallen in love with him! How the hell had that happened? And, now what?

Liz blinked her eyes open. A warm, hard body pressed against her.

Luke.

It all flooded back.

She inched away from him. He didn't stir. She sat up and took deep breaths.

They'd consummated their marriage.

His wavy dark fell onto his forehead, the way she liked it, and hard stubble shadowed his square jawline. She could look at him forever.

She had it bad. She'd even dreamed he told her that he loved her.

How could he?

He deserved someone who wasn't messed up like she was and someone who could trust him.

He'd asked for one night as a condition of the divorce she'd demanded. How could she walk away from him, from this? What would he say to her when he woke up?

He's married to the woman of his dreams, but she hates him with a passion that drives him crazy…

Liz hates Luke for his part in hurting her best friend Amy when he helped *his* best friend Gray to ditch Amy at the altar. But when Liz dares Luke to marry her, while on a drunken romp in Las Vegas, he spirits her away to a wedding chapel before she can back out. Now she's stuck, and he won't give her a divorce unless she spends one night with him, no holds barred…

She wants him as much as he wants her, but she doesn't trust any man…

Liz is blindsided by her attraction to Luke and by his determination to make their Vegas marriage real. But she was assaulted in high school and, although she fought back and escaped, she doesn't trust any man who's not in her immediate family. Now Luke's daring her to trust him with her body and, more importantly, her heart. She's never turned down a dare—but there's never been so much at stake.

KUDOS for *Double Dare*

In *Double Dare* by Tara Eldana, Liz Renfew dares Luke Reddington to marry her while on a drunken romp in Las Vegas. He whisks her off to a wedding chapel before she can change her mind. When she sobers up, she's appalled at what she's done and demands a divorce, but Luke won't give her one. He's crazy about her, even though she hates him for what he helped do to her best friend when *his* best friend left her at the altar. Even though it was a misunderstanding and the two best friends are now happily married, Liz finds herself unable to forgive Luke. Of course the fact that she was assaulted in high school might have something to do with it. After all, Luke is a man, and it was a man who assaulted her. But Luke is determined to win her heart and issues another challenge—knowing she can never resist a dare. This is a cute, sexy, and spicy steamy romance, just my kind of book, and short enough it can easily be read in one sitting. ~ *Taylor Jones, Reviewer*

Double Dare by Tara Eldana is the third steamy romance by this talented author. This time, the story revolves around a young woman who was assaulted the night of her high school prom. Although our heroine, Liz Renfew, escaped with her virginity intact, she came away with a strong distrust of men, a common enough occurrence after an assault. Even though her father and brothers are cops, and they have since taught her to defend herself, she is still afraid to trust Luke Reddington with her heart or her body, even though she dared him to marry her when she was intoxicated, and he did. Now she wants out, but he want to make the marriage real and refuses to let her go. When she won't listen to reason, he dares her to give him just one night, and then he will give her a divorce if she still wants one, and since she is not one to turn down a dare…Like all of Eldana's novellas, *Double Dare* is hot, fun, and sexy. It also deals with issues like the effect a sexual assault can have on a young woman for the rest of her life. A charming story that will warm your heart, make you smile, and have you rooting for the "good" guys. ~ *Regan Murphy, Reviewer*

ACKNOWLEDGEMENTS

To the fabulous staff at Black Opal Books, who work through broken ankles and personal tragedies.

To my husband and family for their support and humor while I do my writing thing.

To the writing family at Black Opal Books and members of the Greater Detroit Romance Writers of America for sharing their knowledge and support.

Double

DARE

Tara Eldana

A Black Opal Books Publication

GENRE: STEAMY ROMANCE/CHICK LIT/WOMEN'S FICTION

This is a work of fiction. Names, places, characters and incidents are either the product of the author's imagination or are used fictitiously, and any resemblance to any actual persons, living or dead, businesses, organizations, events or locales is entirely coincidental. All trademarks, service marks, registered trademarks, and registered service marks are the property of their respective owners and are used herein for identification purposes only. The publisher does not have any control over or assume any responsibility for author or third-party websites or their contents.

DEDICATION

To the good, courageous men and women in law enforcement, who do their jobs because they truly wish to help people, and maintain the thin blue line.

Chapter 1

Liz Renfew's face hurt from stretching it into a phony smile. How could she hate another human being to the depths of her soul the way she hated Luke Reddington? She felt this way even though they stood in a church together as godparents to her best friend Amy and Luke's best friend Gray's twins, Jordan and Jack.

She kept her eyes on Jordan, who she held in her arms. She couldn't, wouldn't look at Luke. She thought he was hot, even though she loathed him with every fiber of her being.

And he was her husband.

He'd married her after she had dared him to in Las Vegas. And the worm wouldn't sign the divorce papers.

Damn Amy for leaving her alone with him and riding off with Gray into the desert moonlight. Her plan was to give Amy a wild girl's night and convince her not to marry Gray. He had left dear, sweet Amy standing at the altar just months before in a whacked-up retaliation for Amy breaking up with his buddy Smitty.

Smitty died soon after—on patrol in Afghanistan, where he, Gray, and Luke were stationed. He had made his relationship with Amy sound much more serious that it was. Amy still had her V-card till she seduced Gray a week before the morning he'd jilted her. And Luke helped him rip Amy's heart out. He drove the getaway car.

Then Luke had the nerve to show up at Amy's place a couple months later to beg Amy to go to Gray, who'd gone off the rails, and talk to him. Amy had caved and gone to him, because she blamed herself for what she believed to be her part in Smitty's death—breaking up with him right before went on his last, fatal patrol, which Amy believed made him reckless or careless. Gray asked her for another chance. And Amy, sweet, loving Amy, did—but not after making him sweat it out.

Liz looked at Amy. She was radiant with her love for Gray and her babies. And Liz had to admit Gray was crazy in love with Amy.

He'd even given her the chance to dump his ass in

front of the minister and their family and friends in Vegas like he did to her, but she didn't.

Liz glared at Luke. He pursed his mouth into a kiss.

She should have shot him when he showed up at Amy's place that day. Her brothers and dad were sheriffs in Emmett County where Amy used to live, which was in Petoskey, near Lake Michigan. Liz had her twenty-two-caliber pistol in her purse and her permit to carry it. Her brothers and dad had taught her how to shoot after her disastrous senior prom night.

Jordan started fussing. She handed the baby to Amy's mom Nancy and was surprised that she immediately missed the smell and feel of the infant in her arms. Luke relinquished Jack to Steve, Amy's dad, and stood next to her. He smelled woodsy.

"How is my darling wife?"

"Shut up. Someone will hear."

"Ashamed of me, baby cakes?"

"Yes. Just sign the damned divorce papers." She flashed Amy a big, fake smile. She hadn't told Amy about that night in Vegas. There never seemed to be a good time. Then Amy had been a smitten newlywed, then pregnant, then sleep-deprived. Amy was looking at them now and frowning.

Why wouldn't he sign the damned papers?

Liz had gotten drunk that night and dared him to marry her.

And he did, although she passed out cold in their hotel room promptly after the ceremony, so nothing had happened.

And now she could only bring herself to release when she thought of him.

∽

Her scent hit him, vanilla and some spice he couldn't name, and he went instantly hard. Fuck. He wasn't signing those damned divorce papers. Not until she gave them a chance. Amy and Gray were with her parents, talking to the priest so he took hold of his wife's waist and hustled her into a small alcove, keeping her back to him. She'd worn her hair down and he remembered it spread out on the pillow on their wedding night.

"I'll sign your damned divorce decree but I have a condition," he whispered in her ear.

She tried to turn to face him but he tightened his hold on her waist so she wouldn't see his obvious erection.

"Spend one night with me—sober."

"That makes zero sense. We didn't consummate it. It's cut and dried."

"Take it or leave it." He nuzzled her neck.

She stood as still as the statue of the Blessed Virgin in the alcove.

Amy called her name and she wrenched herself away from him. "All right. I agree. I just want this over with."

She stared into his eyes. He lifted a strand of her hair.

"Stop that, someone will see."

He nuzzled her neck again. "When, baby cakes?"

Her brown eyes blazed gold. "Stop calling me that. The sooner the better."

"Mmmm." He bit down on her neck. "So eager."

"Hey?" Amy stood at the entrance to the alcove, juggling Jordan and a diaper bag. Her mouth gaped open.

"Later," he said.

ᴄᴧᴇᴧᴓ

Luke stroked Jordan's bonnet as he walked away.

"Holy hell," Amy said.

"That's so wrong, saying it here," Liz said.

Amy handed her the diaper bag. "Do you want to talk about it?"

"Later."

Liz drove back to Amy and Gray's condo and helped with the babies during brunch. Luke held Jack for a time. Watching him with the infant did odd things to her chest and stomach. Needing to focus on something else, she handed Jordan to Amy's mom and started to clean up the dishes.

Her heart thudded in her chest when Luke joined her in the kitchen and handed her dishes to rinse. She clenched her jaw.

They worked well together. What was up with that?

"I know, right?"

He flashed her a shit-eating grin. She fought the urge to grin back. She was so not doing this. He was a heartless jerk, just like that asshole on prom night.

She scowled.

He tapped the tip of her nose. "You look so cute when you scrunch your face up like that."

"Just thinking about Amy's face when you and Gray left her standing alone at the altar. I have a thing about jerks who hurt innocent people."

He frowned, filled the sink with soapy water, and started washing the pots, pans, and casseroles. "Smitty was full of shit. I didn't know that then. Gray told me after."

Just then, Gray hauled a giggling Amy past the kitchen and up the stairs.

"Don't worry, we've got this." Luke's lips quirked into a smile. "He's crazy in love with her, Liz, I mean bat shit crazy. You didn't see him after he left her. It nearly killed him."

She saw a speck of food on the casserole dish that Luke had just washed and dumped it back in the water, which pissed him off.

Good.

He sighed. "I didn't know that Smitty lied. Gray didn't tell me until after. Hell of it is, I still miss the asshole." He rewashed the casserole and set it in the drainer.

"Amy seems to be happy, wouldn't you say?"

She picked up the casserole, which was spotless, and dropped it back in the dishwater.

"That was clean, baby cakes."

"Nu-uh," she said.

He took the clean casserole out of the dish water and sloshed soapy water down the front of her white, lacy blouse.

He smirked. "Oh, sorry."

He rinsed the dish off and set it in the drainer. She took it out, dunked it in the soapy water, and dumped it over his head.

"You'll pay for that baby cakes."

She dunked the dish in the water again and poured it down the front of his pants. "Do. Not. Call. Me. That."

Holy hell. His erection was clearly visible. He followed her stare and laughed. "What do you expect?" He hauled her into his arms like a limp doll.

What was wrong with her? Why did he smell so wonderful?

He traced the outline of her lips with his tongue while he pulled her hard against him.

Did he have any fat at all on his lean, hard frame?

"I'll scream," she said, although she bit back a sigh when his hands moved to her back side to lift her onto the kitchen counter. He wrapped her legs around his waist.

"You will scream my name when I make you come."

He plundered her mouth and his hand slipped under

her skirt then under her thong to her slit. She was wet, damn it, and he groaned. He plunged his tongue in and out as he worked his finger inside her. She did scream, but the noise was muffled by his mouth.

Breathing hard, she stared into his impossibly blue eyes. They were triumphant but tender. He rested his damp forehead on hers.

"My darling wife," he said, smiling.

"Is everything okay?" Amy's mom stood in the doorway. "The babies are down. Oh—"she said, scurrying away.

Liz let loose a string of expletives. She pushed away from him and off the kitchen counter.

Fuck him. Fuck Gray. "And fuck Amy."

He took hold of her shoulders. His blue eyes had gone silver and a muscle near his mouth twitched. He was angry. "Fuck Amy?" he said.

Shit, had she said the last part out loud?

"There's plenty of dishwater here to wash out that mouth of yours." His hands moved to her waist. "I do not like those words on your beautiful lips."

"Tough shit."

He backed her up against the sink, dipped his hand in the dishwater, and covered her mouth with it. "They are happy, Liz. You have to see that. Even though you and I did our best to fuck that up."

She bit his hand hard.

"Fuck."

"So you're allowed to say fuck and I'm not. Fuck that. And I did not try to fuck it up."

She smiled. She'd said fuck three times in twenty seconds.

"You're pissed that Amy gave him another chance. Why?"

He left her and didn't wait for an answer.

Chapter 2

L iz sat on the cold metal bench and stared at the chunks of ice that floated in Lake Michigan. It was a warm day for April and the sun broke free from the cloud cover but she couldn't shake the chill from her bones.

The park was close to the office in Traverse City where she worked doing public relations for the Convention and Visitors Bureau. Her heart wasn't in her job or anything since the twins' christening a month ago.

She hadn't seen or heard from Luke. She'd seen Amy a couple times. Luke, the rat, was right. Amy was crazy in love with Gray.

Am I angry with my friend for giving Gray another chance or am I just envious? No, she wanted Amy to be happy. If Amy wanted Gray, then that was that.

"Hey, Lizzie?"

She jumped.

It was her brother Ron. He sat next to her on the bench, looking handsome in his sheriff's uniform. "I took you by surprise, tsk tsk. You know better."

She pulled her purse, were she kept her .22, close. "No worries, never leave home without it."

"You were miles away, and you were miles away last night at Mom and Dad's. You haven't been yourself for a while, how come?"

"I am so fucked," she said.

He winced. "I hate when you talk like that."

"So does Luke," she said in a small voice. "And you say it all the time."

"Who's he? And I like him already if he hates the way you swear."

She jabbed his arm. "That's so sexist."

"That's not it, Lizzie. Guys hear a girl talk that way and they think she's, well, not who you are."

"Girl, did you say girl? And I am tough. I'll be damned if I let some asshole think he can—"

"What, get close to you? Love you? Cherish you? Every guy is not that torqued-up ass wipe from high school. You're never going to let that happen to you again. You and I and Ryan and Dad made damn sure of that. And that little fucker won't raise his hand to another woman without law enforcement kicking his ass."

She stared at the ice.

"Cut yourself a break, Lizzie. You think you're the only kid to make a bad decision on prom night?" He looked down at her bare feet. "Test the water with who-ever this guy is who doesn't want you to swear. What's his name, by the way?"

"Luke Reddington. Two Ds." She knew he would check him out.

"For one real minute, I dare you to stick your foot in that lake. I dare you."

He knew she couldn't resist a dare. Apparently nei-ther could Luke.

Her eyes filled with tears.

"What the hell, Lizzie, you never cry." He put his arm around her. "Tell me what's going on right now," he said in his tough cop voice.

She sobbed out her story with her head on his shoul-der.

He frowned. "Describe this guy. What's he look like?"

She did then moved out of his arms. "Don't you have work?"

It was only two and his shift ended at three. His walkie talkie crackled.

"You jinxed it." He smiled. "We'll talk later." He hugged her.

"This guy, Luke, he's into you Lizzie. Seriously. No guy gets married to prove a point."

He sprinted across the sand toward his squad car.

෫ඁඁෑ

Fuck.

Luke could see even from across the parking lot that the fucking cop had his hands on her. Luke's brain detached from his body, and he was halfway to the bench, thinking how he would pull her out of his arms and plant his fist in his face when he remembered something she said.

He'd shown up at Amy's and begged her to go to Gray. Liz said she had a gun, and she could shoot him because her brothers and dad were sheriffs, and they'd taught her how.

The cop ran across the sand. He had the same brown hair and eyes that Liz did. The receptionist in Convention and Visitors Bureau office said she was taking a late lunch in the park by the beach. Her office wasn't far from his and Gray's office.

The cop stopped short in front of him. "Luke, right?" His walkie-talkie-type thing crackled that some unit was responding to something. "I'm Ron. We've got about five seconds before Lizzie sees us." His lips quirked into a quick smile. "You married her on a dare?"

How much had she told him?

Ron shrugged. "She talks tough and she is, but—"

"I know. She's sweet. I get that."

"She's been hurt, and she has trust issues."

"Hurt?" Luke would kill the guy. "Who?"

"Not that way. The jerk wad slapped her around on prom night when she turned him down. She got away and we've got his ass covered. Trust me."

"What's his name?"

"Evan Rocher. He lives downstate now."

She noticed them then, picked up her shoes and purse, and ran toward them.

"You want a chance with her, right? She can't turn down a dare, ever."

She reached them and grabbed her brother's arm.

"Got to run, Lizzie." Ron hugged her fast then ran to his squad car.

"Fucking coward," she said.

Luke took hold of her chin. "One kiss for every filthy word out of that sweet mouth." He kept it light and gentle, although he wanted to sink down in the sand and bury himself inside her.

He pulled away and stared into her wary eyes.

"I didn't agree to that."

He kept hold of her chin. "Have dinner with me tonight."

"I've got to get back."

His fingers traced the line of her jaw. "Have dinner. With me. Tonight. I dare you."

Her eyes danced. "I get to pick."

"Of course. I've got your cell."

"Damn Amy."

He bent to kiss her. She evaded him. "Damn doesn't count."

She ran away from him, clutching her shoes and purse. He sucked in a breath. Did she realize she agreed to his swearing rule?

Liz picked a diner out of the city, a place the tourists didn't know about. Her uncle Stu and Aunt Debbie owned it. They hugged her then looked at him in question.

"This is Luke."

He grinned and put his arm around her.

Stu and Debbie shared a look then gave them a prized booth in the crowded restaurant.

He slid in the seat next to her. "This place is packed on a Tuesday night. The nearest town is forty miles away."

She shrugged. "I know."

∽∾∽∾

Her aunt sat behind the counter and stared at her cell phone, likely texting Liz's mother who had probably already heard about Luke from Ron—the traitor.

A text came in from her mother.

Call me tomorrow.

Luke turned his face into her neck.

"Everything okay?" His mouth was close to her ear.

She made a half-hearted move to pull away. "Don't."

Another text came from her mom.

First thing.

Turning his head, he picked up a menu and put his hand on her thigh. Why had she worn a skirt? She didn't bother with a menu.

If she grabbed his wrist to stop him, he would know his touch was affecting her. She struggled to keep her breath even.

"What do you want?" he breathed into her ear.

The sound of his voice alone could seduce her. She leaned away from him, grabbed a napkin from the dispenser, and crunched it into a ball in her sweaty hand.

He moved his other arm to the back of the bench then to her shoulders. "What do you want, baby cakes?"

"Don't call me that."

He moved his hand higher to the apex of her thighs. She sucked in a breath.

"What do you want, sweet wife?"

Her Aunt Debbie stood at their table, her mouth agape. He looked down at his menu.

"Wife?" Aunt Debbie mouthed then turned on her heel back to the counter.

He pressed his arm around her shoulders. Liz's phone pinged.

Her mother. *WIFE!!! Call me now.*

"Let me out."

She grabbed her phone and stepped outside. It was dark and the sky was filled with stars. Her talk with her mom was mercifully brief, surprising because her mom was relentless when she was on a mission to get information. She told her mom they would talk on the weekend.

Liz walked back to the table, to find Luke in earnest conversation with her Uncle Stu about the Detroit Tigers. She slid in next to him, offering her take on the pitching lineup. Her uncle squeezed her hand and slid out of the booth.

"The usual, Lizzie?"

She nodded. "He'll have the same."

Her uncle left them, chuckling. Luke didn't touch her, which puzzled her. It would look dumb if she got up and sat across from him. Why did she miss his touch?

"She knows baseball." His smile warmed her.

She shrugged. "Two brothers and Karen and Dan for parents."

"Let's go to a game. This weekend. They're playing the Yankees."

"As if. You can't get tickets."

He clutched his heart. "You wound me. One of the guys we do business with has season tickets he can't use. He has to go to an out of town wedding with his wife. He's pissed."

"Hell, yes."

He raised his eyebrows and claimed her lips in a hard, fast kiss.

"Hell doesn't count," she said.

"I just wanted to kiss you."

Her toes curled. What was wrong with her?

※※※

Liz shivered as the early May night air rolled into Comerica Park. The Tigers pulled it off in the bottom of the ninth, three-to-two. The sky lit up with the fireworks since it was a Saturday night game. Luke had driven them down from Traverse City that morning. They hit Greektown for lunch and the Detroit Institute of Arts before the game. She'd turned down his offer of dinner in a restaurant for ball park hot dogs and beer.

She had no idea where they were spending the night. He said it was a surprise. The fireworks ended and she shivered through the light sweater she wore over the official Tiger shirt he'd bought her. He put his coat over her shoulders.

He held her hand till they reached the spot where he'd parked his Charger. "Let's grab a drink before we head home."

"Home?"

"Not Traverse. Here. I'm from Royal Oak. There's a bar right by my mom's house."

He made a series of turns till he was driving north on

Woodward, the first paved street in the country, then pulled into the parking lot of a non-descript bar. She pulled her gun out of the glove box and slipped it back into her purse. He threaded his fingers through hers and led her inside.

It was a typical dive bar with a long row of bar stools and few tables. P&L's Bar and Lounge. She loved it.

He held out a chair for her as she looked around then froze. She grabbed her purse and reached inside.

It was Evan.

He stood by the pool table.

Chapter 3

We can leave," Luke said, disappointed she didn't like it.

She didn't answer him. His mother was good friends with the owners, their neighbors, Lori and Pete. They refused to change the look of their no-frills bar to look like all the other bars that dotted this stretch of Woodward.

His mother had worked a shift or two here when money was tight while Luke watched TV or did his homework in Pete's office.

Pete stood behind the bar.

"I have to say hi to someone, then we can leave…"

Luke's voice trailed off. Liz stared at some dude playing pool and she had her hand in her purse. She looked ill. He squeezed her shoulders. "What's wrong, baby?"

"Evan Rocher," she whispered.

"From prom night?"

She nodded, never taking her eyes away from the pool table as she pulled her gun out of her purse.

Rage and the instinct to put his hands on the piece of shit who hurt her propelled Luke across the bar.

He'd kill the fucker.

He got between Rocher and the pool table.

Rocher stepped back. "What the fuck?"

Pete was looking at them. Rocher's fat arms were covered in tats, and his gut spilled over his jeans.

Rocher saw Liz then. She flinched.

"Don't fucking look at her."

"Who the fuck are you? I'll look at that bitch if I want."

"Her husband." Luke punched him in the face then pummeled anything he could make contact with.

Rocher's fist connected with Luke's chin, and he felt metal pierce his skin. He landed a blow to Rocher's temple and kicked his foot, unbalancing him. Rocher fell hard on the floor.

Luke followed him down and got his hands around his neck.

"Let him go."

Liz stood over them, her gun trained on Rocher's

chest. Luke smelled piss and saw that Rocher had wet himself.

"This isn't your fight. Let me finish it." Her voice was dead calm.

The guy Rocher had been playing pool with ran out of there with his cell phone in his hand.

A guy at the bar nudged Pete. "Dude's bleeding."

"You can't let this bitch kill me."

Luke's hands tightened around Rocher's neck, choking off his pleas.

Sirens sounded. Pete stepped out from behind the bar and put his hand on Luke's shoulder. "You'll kill him, son." Then he turned to Liz. "Give me the gun, sweetheart."

She waited a long moment then handed him her gun. Luke lessened his hold on Rocher's neck. The sirens wailed.

"Any of you assholes see anything?" Pete hollered.

A collective "No" rang out.

"Let me do the talking," Pete said.

He set the safety, put the gun behind the bar, came back, and stood over Rocher. Luke let Rocher go and went to Liz. Her eyes were glazed, and she was pale and trembling. He folded her into his arms, and Pete handed him a napkin for his bleeding chin.

Two policemen burst through the door. The older officer stepped to where Rocher was sprawled on the floor. "Someone pull a gun, Pete?"

"Naw. I was just about to call you guys to get this asshole out of here. I cut him off, and he started a fight." Pete pointed at Rocher and the younger cop cuffed him.

The older cop looked around the bar. "That what happened?"

Everyone nodded.

"I—It was h—her," Rocher sputtered. He sneered at Liz. "Bitch was going to shoot me."

The older officer frowned. "Miss, I need to check you and your purse."

Liz pushed away from Luke. "Sure. My dad and brothers are sheriffs. I know how this works."

"What's your name, miss?"

"Liz Renfew. Dan's my dad. He's in Emmett County."

"Danny? We played golf at a conference last year. He owes me a beer. Just open your purse."

She did and the younger officer searched it. "Nothing." he said.

He looked at his partner, and Luke gritted his teeth at the thought of him putting his hands on her. The older officer nodded, and his partner started to pat her down.

The older officer stepped between Luke and Liz. "You know this young lady, before tonight?"

"She's my wife."

"I need to search you, sir."

"Sure."

The older cop patted him down then stepped back.

"Wife?" Pete chuckled. "Patty never said." He held a cell phone in his hand.

"She doesn't know."

Pete held up his phone. "She does now."

The older cop glanced around the bar. "Anyone want to make a statement?"

Everyone stayed quiet.

Rocher pointed to Pete. "She gave the gun to him."

Pete stepped forward and the younger cop patted him down.

"He went behind the bar," Rocher said.

"Go ahead," Pete said.

The older cop looked behind the bar.

"What's your name, so I can tell Dad?" Liz asked him.

"Art Buchanan."

"Artie? He's mentioned you." She pointed at Rocher but didn't look at him. "That asshole attacked my husband."

Luke loved hearing her call him her husband.

"We just got married." She stepped toward him, and he plastered her to his side, keeping his napkin on his chin.

Artie gestured to Rocher. "Do you know this guy?"

"No," she said.

Luke tightened his hold on her as they read Rocher his Miranda rights then led him away.

Pete lifted up a floor tile under the bar, took the gun

out, wrapped it in a bar rag. "Going to Patty's, I hope?"

"Yeah," Luke said.

"Take this, you'll need it. She's going to kill you for getting married without her being there."

⋘⋙

Liz shook as she slid behind the wheel of Luke's Charger and moved the seat up. A huge hospital loomed ahead. She drove toward it.

"No." Luke squeezed her arm and put the gun in her purse. "Turn right after the light."

"You need stitches," she said.

"One stitch, maybe, and Patty can do it."

"You call your mom Patty?"

"Not to her face."

She made the turn then two more, per Luke's instructions.

"I'm sorry you got mixed up in my shit."

"Kissable offense. You owe me, and your shit is my shit now, my darling wife."

She shivered, but not from the cold as they walked toward a two story bungalow.

A woman with Luke's blue eyes and wavy brown hair threw the door open and scowled at Luke.

"Married, you're married?" she shrieked.

"Hi, Mom," he said. "I'd kiss you but I'm bleeding."

She waved him off and stepped toward Liz, wrapping her in a hug. "I'm Patty, your husband's mother."

She smelled like cherry chip cake. "Come inside."

Patty kept her arm around Liz, ignoring her son.

"Bleeding here," he said.

"Pete texted," Patty said. "Keep the pressure on. And get my stuff. It's in my bedroom." She smiled and drew Liz onto a leather sofa. "Sit down. I'm not mad at you, sweetie. But Lucas needs to feel my wrath."

Patty chatted easily and Liz told her about her job, growing up in Traverse City, and that her dad and brothers were sheriffs.

Patty smiled. "What do you carry?"

Luke sat across from them.

"A .22," Liz said.

Patty nodded. "So do I. I go through some tough neighborhoods." She took the medical bag from Luke. "I'm an RN and I volunteer. Kitchen, sit," she said to Luke.

Liz followed and watched Patty clean his gash and put a drop of what looked like glue on it, while she talked about how determined Luke had been to play baseball although she could barely afford it.

She chatted about his record on the high school varsity team then in college at Central Michigan University, where he'd apparently gone on a baseball scholarship, as if Liz knew all about it.

"How many teams are you on now?" Patty said.

Luke kept his eyes on Liz. "Two."

"This one may scar," Patty said. "He's been clipped with a bat a few times."

"I'll grow a beard."

"No," Liz and Patty said in unison. Patty stroked his jawline. "It's a sin to hide this."

His eyes blazed into Liz's. She looked away. She felt too raw and exposed.

"Change your sheets, Luke. They're dusty."

Patty watched him disappear down the hall. "I take it this was sudden. He never gives up, sweetie. Not when it's something or someone he wants." She squeezed Liz's hand. "I'm turning in. See you in the morning."

Chapter 4

A warm, hard body pressed against her back and an arm held her around her waist. She blinked her eyes open.

Luke.

Her temporary husband.

She was in his bed in the house where he grew up.

The sun blazed through the blinds. She'd dropped off as soon as her head hit the pillow. She looked around his room. He stirred then and pulled her harder against him.

"Hmmmm," he said against her ear. His erection pressed into her backside. "I didn't dream you."

"You dream me?"

"Since the first time I saw you," he said.

When was that? It had to be at Gray and Amy's wedding rehearsal when he knew damn well that he would help Gray rip Amy's heart out the next day. Liz had to remember that. She wrenched away from him.

"It was fucked up, baby, I know that."

He stood up, magnificently nude. She wanted to slide her hands over his six pack abs then lower to his thick, erect cock. She squeezed her eyes shut as desire coursed through her. He stood behind her, lifted her hair, and sucked her hard on her neck. She knew it would leave a mark.

She bit back a moan.

"Offer stands, my darling wife. One night." His hands moved to her breasts, pulling them free from the bra she'd slept in. He teased her nipples to stiff points. "One night, no Smitty bullshit, no lies, just us. If you can walk away, then I'll sign whatever you want."

What did she want?

Patty rattled pots and pans.

"Mom's being subtle. This isn't over, babe. Not by a long shot." He grabbed her hand led her to the bathroom. She showered first, dried her hair, and dressed in the bedroom while he showered. He took her hand again and they went into the kitchen.

"Hope you like pancakes," Patty said.

"Chocolate chip?" he asked.

"Of course."

He stood behind his mother and kissed her on her cheek.

Liz looked away, feeling like she was intruding, wandered into the living room, and studied the framed photos. Most were of Luke in baseball uniforms. The first one must have been when he was seven or eight. He looked so determined.

"I was."

She jumped. Had she spoken out loud? He stood behind her.

"Coach wanted me to play third base. I wanted first."

"Did you?"

His hands came around her waist.

"Yeah. I don't give up when it's something I want." He nuzzled her neck. "This, us, is all I can think about."

Patty said he didn't give up.

"Shit."

"Language." He turned her in his arms and kissed her. It was a light, teasing kiss. His tongue flirted with hers.

Smelling bacon, she pulled away. Her stomach rumbled.

"Can I help?" she called out.

"Sure, hon, set the table. Luke, could you take a look at the motion light on the patio?"

Luke stepped outside and Liz stood in front of the cupboards. "Where are the plates?"

Patty pointed and poured pancake batter into the fry

pan. "Straight up, sweetie, what's the deal? You love each other, and you're married. I heard what Luke just said. I guess I'm being a meddling mother-in-law. Sorry."

Holy hell. And Liz detected a slight southern accent she hadn't heard before.

"My Texas comes out when I get nervous," Patty said. "Luke's dad and I came up from Waco when he took a job with Chrysler. He's been gone a long time. Pancreatic cancer. Luke was little."

"I'm so sorry," Liz said.

"He's like his dad. He loves a girl with spunk." Patty winked. "But you all seem stuck."

Luke came back before Liz could form an answer.

He devoured two plates. The bacon was perfectly crisp but not dry and the pancakes exploded with chocolate. Patty shared neighborhood gossip as they finished their coffee.

Why had she never remarried? She had to be in her late forties, but didn't look to be out of her thirties. He'd never shared anything about his family. But they'd never had a serious conversation about their lives. She was curious but hesitant to get more tangled up with a man she wanted to cut out of her life.

That *was* what she wanted, right?

ຕະ

The bouquets were different every day. They were

delivered to her office or apartment—long-stemmed red roses, daisies, sunflowers and some she didn't recognize. The card always said the same thing: One night.

Amy was out for a rare visit without Jack and Jordan. Nana and Papa took the twins for the afternoon. Liz and Amy braved the tourist crowds to go Saturday shopping and to lunch and then were back at her apartment. Amy was sniffing the bouquets.

Luke and Gray were on a business trip in Fort Wayne and were due back that night. Amy picked up one of the cards and read it out loud.

"One night, holy hell, Liz. What happened in Vegas didn't stay there, I'm thinking."

"You mean the night you ditched me for Gray?"

Amy's face crumpled.

"I didn't mean it, Ames." Liz sighed. Amy and Gray were crazy in love. Liz knew that. She took a deep breath. "He married me, Ames. I dared him to and then he dared me back."

"Shit. You can't turn down a dare."

"We got stupid crazy drunk after. We woke up in bed together, but nothing happened. I am so pissed at him for what he did to you."

"What Gray did to me because Smitty lied?"

"I want a divorce. And he wants one night. After that he says he'll do whatever I want."

Liz grabbed a couple beers from her fridge and they drank them in silence.

Her cell phone pinged with a text.

It was from Luke.

"Tonight. Your place. I dare you."

"Fuck." She held her phone so Amy could see.

"You will be. Fucked, I mean." Amy giggled. "He's sex on a stick, girlfriend. Have your way with him then walk away, if that's what you want. He's a good guy, though. He went to Central on a baseball scholarship and joined the reserves to pay off his loans. He met Gray overseas."

Amy's phone pinged. "Oooh, they're back." Her phone rang. "I'm in Traverse at Liz's place." She looked at Liz and blushed. "Isn't Luke there? No, my parents wanted them all afternoon. We have till six." She made wide eyes at Liz and bit her lip. "Let's do something together, all four of us."

Liz heard Gray laugh through the phone.

Amy giggled. "No, she will not shoot him."

Liz shook her head. "Go have monkey sex with your hot husband."

"No, this is our time."

"Out, now. I have stuff to do."

Amy got flustered at something Gray said. Liz handed Amy her purse, bags, and keys. "Go."

Liz shut her door and thought about hiding out for the night. That way, she wouldn't be turning down the dare. She could go up to Mackinaw, take the ferry to the island, and spend the night there. The Convention and

Visitors Bureau kept a standing room available at the Grand Hotel. She could spend the night sipping wine on the long elegant porch—alone.

So what if he'd dared her? She wasn't ready. She would never be ready. She grabbed some underwear, her makeup bag, hair stuff, the Detroit Tigers baseball shirt Luke bought her at the stadium, a short, clingy red dress she loaned to Amy for their bust of a wild night in Vegas, and Fuck-me three-inch heels. She stuffed it all in a rucksack, grabbed her purse and keys, and ran out her front door—smack into Luke.

e∕ɔe∕ɔ

Thank fuck he hadn't gone to his place first.

"Baby cakes, you disappoint me. Running away from a dare."

She shoved her phone in her rucksack. "What are you talking about?"

"My text."

"What text?"

She wore a lacy tank top and jeans that hugged her backside. He lifted her chin and traced the outline of her soft pink lips with his finger. "You're a shit liar."

He pushed her back against her door and traced her lips with his tongue. She dropped her rucksack and purse to the floor. He speared his fingers through her soft, dark hair.

She turned her face away and he nuzzled her neck. She smelled like vanilla.

"I am not."

"Yes, babe, you are."

She softened against him and he pressed his advantage, fusing his mouth to hers. She tasted like beer and heaven and home. He lifted her so she hung in his arms. Her hands crept around his neck and she raked her fingernails into his scalp. He deepened the kiss. His erection pressed against her sex.

He slipped his hand under the waist band of her jeans then lower to her slit, stroking her sweet pearl. She bucked against him and tore her mouth away.

"Stop," she panted.

Her eyes were dilated and her lips were swollen from his kisses. She grabbed his arm.

He plunged his fingers into her tight channel. She was soaked. "Why, baby?"

She gripped his arm. "We're in a hallway. Anyone could see."

He pulled his fingers, coated with her juices, and pressed them against her soft lips.

"Suck. Taste how you want me." Her eyes went wide but she did it. He dropped his forehead to hers. "Let's go inside, baby."

She wiggled away from him. "Not here."

He took hold of her waist and tried to process her words. Did that mean she wanted him, just not here? She was pliant in his arms. It took every ounce of his control not to break her door down and ravage her against the wall. He had to slow the fuck down.

"Where, baby?" he murmured against her ear, turning her around, and pulling her back against his chest. "Where you want to go?"

He trailed kisses down her jawline to her neck. She tilted her head, giving him access to the spot he loved near her shoulder. He bit down on the tendon and she arched her back. He splayed his hand on her stomach and she sucked in a breath. His cock pressed into the sweet curve of her butt. He had to go slow or he'd fuck this up.

"Where, baby?" He looked down at her rucksack and tamped town his temper. She was running away from him, from this. He kept his voice soft. 'Where were you going, baby?"

He moved his hand lower to her sex. She shuddered. Thank fuck. She was still with him.

"Mackinaw," she whimpered. "The ferry to the island. Work has a room at the Grand. I took it for tonight."

"That's good, baby."

His dick was so hard that it could cut glass but he would drive them to the dock, take the ferry, check them into the hotel, and get her naked. He could do this. He'd faced enemy fire in Afghanistan. If she wanted him to make love to her on Mackinaw Island, he could tame his raging dick and wait.

"I'll drive, baby. All my stuff is in my car."

ↄ⁄ↄↄ⁄ↄ

The air off Lake Huron chilled Liz's skin as the ferry skittered across the waves to Mackinaw Island. He held her hand. She hadn't said much on the drive but he'd touched her in some way since they left her apartment.

Why had she agreed to the one night he wanted? Could she walk away from him? Why was he insisting on this? She'd threatened his life and she'd meant it.

"That's sexy as hell," he said.

"What?"

"You and your little gun."

"Shit. I've got to stop thinking out loud."

"Please don't."

He kissed her hard. The ferry slowed and maneuvered into the dock. He grabbed her bag and his own and followed her down the gang plank, keeping a hand on the small of her back. They boarded a horse-drawn trolley to the hotel and laughed at the driver's jokes about horse poop. The only motorized vehicles on the island were the snowmobiles the year-round residents used to get to the towns on the mainland when the Lake Huron froze over.

She gave her name to the hotel clerk and rummaged through her wallet for her credit card, since the room was discounted but not free, but Luke took care of it. He waved the bell hop off and took their bags to their room. She slid the keycard in, pushed the door open, and he dropped their bags on the floor.

She started inside. But he put his hands on her waist, stopping her.

"Huh?"

He grinned, swung her up in his arms, carried her into the room, and put her on the bed. Then he picked up their bags and dropped them near the bathroom.

He'd just carried her over the threshold. Holy hell.

She scooted off the bed and picked up the phone. He stood, watching her.

"We shouldn't have a problem with a dinner reservation." Her words came out in a rush.

He hadn't shaved. Stubble shadowed his movie star jawline. She'd seen more than one woman go slack-jawed looking at him today. He took the phone out of her nerveless fingers.

He reached for her hand and brought it to his lips. "Are you hungry, baby?"

Why did he have to be so mouth-watering handsome and, in turns, so sweet? He was confusing her. He was cold-hearted. She forced herself to think of Amy standing at her wedding, watching Gray and Luke walk away. Liz would have taken aim at Luke then if she'd had her gun. She felt faint.

She shook with nerves. Gray had left her best friend at the altar, not Luke. Why did she feel as if Luke betrayed her?

"Baby, what's wrong?" He eased her back on the bed, elevated her feet, and then pressed a cold compress to her forehead. He took her pulse, picked up the phone, and ordered room service appetizers. He poured her a glass of water and held it to her lips.

"You're good at this," she said.

"Patty. You need anything else, baby?"

He pressed the cloth to her forehead.

She swallowed hard. "My gun." He raised his eyebrows. She shrugged. "Could you put it in the safe? And take it when we leave. I shouldn't have it."

He took it from her purse and looked at her in question. She couldn't keep it. Her blood ran too hot when she was near him. He pressed the safe shut and held the key out.

"No. You keep it."

"Why, baby?"

To her horror, tears threatened. "You, us."

He sank down on the bed and took her in his arms. "Don't cry, I can't stand it." He turned her face to his. "Makes me want to mess up whoever hurt you. In this case, I'm thinking it's me."

He rested his forehead on hers and set the safe key on the nightstand.

The food came then and he fed her bites of chicken and bacon wrapped sausage, batting her hands away when she tried to feed herself. He dipped chunks of pita bread in a chickpea sauce. She nibbled that between bites of chicken and sausage.

Feeling stuffed, she waved him away. He cleaned up

the dishes and set them outside the door. He put the safe key into his pocket and held out his hand. "Let's grab a seat on the porch for sunset."

She let out her breath she hadn't realized she was holding. She took his hand and stood, feeling clear head-ed.

What had she expected? That he would jump on top of her as soon as she swallowed her last chicken wing?

Chapter 5

The line "I can see the sunset in your eyes," from the Peter Frampton song, "Baby, I Love Your Ways," that Patty loved, played in his head as they sat on the Victorian-style porch the hotel was known for. He held her hand as the sun dipped into Lakes Huron and Michigan, shining off the Mackinaw Bridge that connected the mitten part of the state to the Upper Peninsula where Gray had gone off the rails after he abandoned Amy at the altar.

And Luke had helped Gray abandon and humiliate Amy because Gray felt he owed it to Smitty to hurt her. Gray blamed her for breaking Smitty's heart so he got careless on that last patrol or just wanted to die. And Luke had Gray's back, always.

Luke traced the veins in her wrist. Would she ever forgive him? "I'm sorry, baby."

She looked puzzled.

"About my part in the shit day. Even if all of the bullshit lies about him and Amy were true, I had no right to judge anybody."

The sun dropped into the water.

"Nothing was going to bring him back," he said.

She squeezed his hand.

Taking a deep breath, Luke continued. "Gray was more messed up than I was. They offer you help but no one takes it. We're Marines—you know, the code. Gray loved Amy from the first time he saw her, love at first sight. Smitty saw it, and the asshole snagged her first. He was so damned jealous of Gray."

"I never knew," she said.

She'd moved in with Amy into an apartment when they were juniors and Amy's roommate had ditched her and left her with the lease.

"You came later. After Smitty and Gray were there two years."

They sat without speaking for a bit.

"I love this time of day—night, I guess." He squeezed her hand. "It's like anything's possible."

The light reflected off the water. She shivered. He pulled her onto his lap and pressed his face into her neck.

"Is it, baby? Is anything possible?"

She pressed against him.

∽∾∽

After Evan and her disastrous prom night, Liz had tried to date, but she didn't want sex with any of the guys she'd gone out with, and, once they figured that out, they didn't stick around. She got on birth control right after Evan assaulted her, but she was still a virgin.

Now she felt soft and boneless in Luke's arms.

Was this possible?

"I've never done this."

He lifted her chin. "I know, baby. You told me in Vegas."

"I did?"

He kissed her. His tongue teased her lips open. She clung to him.

Could she trust him? Could she trust any man?

He pulled his mouth away from her and held her as it got darker. She was sick of Evan's attack ruling her life. Had she held onto her anger at Luke as a shield?

"I don't know how much my brother told you, but after Evan attacked me on prom night, I saw a therapist for a while. I lived at home and went to community college, but I got sick of rehashing it. It gave him too much power, you know?"

He kissed the top of her forehead. "Yeah, baby, I

know. Mom took me to someone, a nice lady, for a while after Dad died because she thought I was depressed. I was pissed that he left us. I guess I didn't think he fought it hard enough. I was a dumb kid. It was pancreatic cancer, nearly impossible to beat. It's hard to be pissed at someone who dies. You get sick of talking about it."

She kissed him then, tracing his lips with her tongue. He deepened the kiss and she shivered. His tongue plunged deeply in and out and she met him thrust for thrust. He released her and rested his head on her forehead. His breath was warm and sweet.

"Yes, Luke. Anything is possible."

"My sweet wife." He slid her off his lap and stood, lacing his fingers through hers. He didn't speak till they were back in the room. He hung the "Do Not Disturb" sign on the door then pulled his shirt off. He backed her against the wall, took hold of her waist, and claimed her mouth. She hung in his arms. He slid his fingers in her hair and caressed her scalp.

He turned his face into her neck. "You. Are. So. Sweet. I'm clean, baby. There's been no one else since Vegas. Are you on birth control?"

"Yes, since Evan," she said.

He lifted his head. The light left his eyes. "I would have killed him that night at Pete's. He put his hands on you, then you felt you had to pretend to be someone you're not." He smiled, and the iciness left his, eyes making them the warm blue she loved.

Loved?

"You're smart and strong and brave," he whispered.

She pulled his head down and kissed him, trying to show him what she couldn't put in words. Her lips left his mouth and trailed down his muscled chest to his flat nipples.

She teased first one, then its twin with her tongue. He moaned and everything fell away except the magnetic pull this man, her husband, had on her body, her mind, and her heart.

How had that happened?

He growled and moved them to the bed. She caressed him, letting her hands roam over his chest and washboard abs. He pulled her clothes off, unhooked her bra, and then slid her panties slowly down her thighs. He stood and took his pants and boxers off, leaving their clothes in piles on the floor.

He rolled her beneath him and her hands gripped his waist, then lower to his rock hard butt. He grabbed each hand and imprisoned them over her head.

"I want to make this good for you, baby, but if you keep that up, I won't last."

His cock nudged the opening of her damp slit and his thumb found her clit. She writhed under his touch until she came, screaming his name. His eyes never left her face.

"I've always used a condom but I want you bareback so bad I can't see straight." He released her hands and stroked her cheek. "So this is a first for me, too. Do you trust me?"

Doubt bubbled up. He hurt Amy, or helped Gray to hurt her. Would he turn his back on her after tonight and give her the divorce she said she wanted? He said he wanted one night. He'd said all that other stuff, but didn't guys say anything at this point to get what they wanted?

He wanted her, at least right now.

"I've got to give up my V-card sometime." She regretted her sarcastic tone and words the instant she'd said them.

The light left his eyes again and she wanted to bring it back.

"Stop hiding behind that don't fuck with me attitude and don't belittle this, or us."

She smiled. "You said fuck."

His eyes lit up again and his lips quirked into a smile. "You just repeated it, knowing the penalty."

"So I did." She squirmed underneath him and caressed the stubble on his jaw with her now free hand. "I trust you." And in that moment she did, with her body and her heart.

He lowered his mouth to her sex. She gasped. He laughed. "I take my penalty kisses wherever and whenever. Utter at your own peril or, I hope, pleasure."

He sucked on her clit and slipped one, then two fingers inside her, finding her G-spot. She'd never allowed this intimacy with anyone before. He sucked hard and she saw stars. He entered her in one hard thrust, pushing past her barrier, all her barriers.

"I'm sorry, I'm sorry, I'm sorry," he said.

"Don't be," she said. Her tissues stretched to accommodate his fullness. She felt complete. "It was just a pinch."

He pulled out then filled her again. He looked at her as if she was more important to him than his next breath. "Keep your eyes open."

∽∾∽

He forced himself to go slow. With sweet, trusting eyes, she raised her hips each time he plunged into her.

"I won't break," she said.

He pressed his thumb over her clit and pounded into her. Did she know how responsive she was? And what a hair trigger she was for him?

She moaned and he stopped. "Am I hurting you?"

"No." Her chocolate brown eyes shone with gold lights, tiger eyes. Her nails dug into his back, marking him. "Don't stop, please."

He reentered her in one stroke, hitting her sweet spot. She said his name in two long syllables. Her eyes were wide open but unfocused. A bead of sweat formed on her upper lip. He licked it off. Her skin felt like silk everywhere.

"I want us to go together," he said.

"I'm close, please don't stop."

"Never."

He slammed into her, his brain separating from his body. He emptied himself inside her, draining his balls and she screamed his name. He collapsed on top of her for a few moments then rolled them on their sides, still inside her tight channel.

He stroked her hair, murmuring nonsensical words, before he eased out of her and got a damp washcloth to clean her, them himself. The sheet was stained with her virgin's blood. He stared, burning the image into his brain. He would take the sheet with him when they left and launder it himself so nobody else would see her sacred gift.

She snored softly and he chuckled, pressing his front to her back.

"I love you," he said close to her ear.

She sighed, then resumed snoring.

What would she say if he said the words when she was awake? Could he? She had to know how he felt about her, didn't she?

Her drunken dare that he marry her was a gift from the heavens. He'd hustled her sweet ass out of that meat market bar on the strip and to the first wedding chapel he could find.

She slept so sweetly in his arms that night. He never shut his eyes, fighting a raging hard on and guilt that she deserved a no-holds-barred wedding with the people she loved around her, not a hokey ceremony in a cheesy chapel.

But he would not let her go without a fight.

Would she come to love him the way he loved her? Could she love any man after the way that animal brutalized her? Could he accept whatever crumbs she could give him?

He pressed his nose into her hair. Her sweet vanilla smell called to a part of him he'd never known existed, calming and exciting him in equal parts.

Chapter 6

Liz blinked her eyes open. A warm, hard body pressed against her.

Luke.

It all flooded back.

She inched away from him. He didn't stir. She sat up and took deep breaths.

They'd consummated their marriage.

His wavy dark fell onto his forehead, the way she liked it, and hard stubble shadowed his square jawline. She could look at him forever.

She had it bad. She'd even dreamed he told her that he loved her.

How could he?

He deserved someone who wasn't messed up like she was and someone who could trust him.

He'd asked for one night as a condition of the divorce she'd demanded. How could she walk away from him, from this? What would he say to her when he woke up?

She loved him.

Somewhere between the Vegas strip, doing christening dishes at Amy's house, and the seventh-inning stretch at Comerica Park, she fell in love with him.

She had to get away to think.

Doing a quick wash in the bathroom sink, reluctant to wash off his scent, she dressed in the Tigers T-shirt, he'd gotten for her at the ballpark, and jeans. She skipped makeup, pulled her hair into a messy pony tail, grabbed her purse, forgetting her rucksack with her birth control pills, and shut the door as softly as she could.

She checked her phone. It was seven-thirty. Could she make the first ferry back?

*ભ*ભ*ભ

The door snapped shut and Luke blinked his eyes awake. She was gone. He sat up and dragged his hand through his hair. Her rucksack was next to the door. He could see her birth control pills on the top of her stuff. He expelled a breath.

Thank fuck. She was coming back, right? Unless she just forgot it in her rush to leave him. She'd given him what he demanded for the divorce she wanted.

Did she still want it? The words to a Bonnie Raitt song Pete played in the bar, "I can't make you love me," played over and over in his head.

Perfect.

She did love him, he knew it. She was just scared to trust him. He picked up her rucksack. Would she come back for it? He picked up her pack of pills. He knew that ideally, they should be taken at the same time every day from the house calls he went on with Patty and the work she did at women's shelters. He remembered she'd swallowed something with coffee that morning at Patty's house.

He was a rat bastard, a desperate rat bastard. He slipped her pills into his bag then stripped the stained sheet off the bed, unclipped the laundry bag and stuffed it inside. He stashed that in his bag, too. Locking the door so she couldn't get back in without knocking, he stepped under the cold spray of the shower, scraping the razor over his face because she said she liked him clean shaven.

He pulled his clothes on. It was just after eight o'clock.

Should he wait here in case she came back or wait at the dock? Depending on when the first ferry left, she could already be gone.

But she would need a ride when she got to the mainland. She could call her family for a ride. He looked at his phone, scrolled to her number, and hit call.

Game on.

⌒⌒

Damn.

She forgot her overnight bag, and it time to take her pill. The ferry was boarding. She stepped out of the line. The stiff breeze off the water chilled her arms and face. Her phone rang.

It was Luke. Her heart lurched.

Was he pissed?

Had she destroyed their fragile bond by running away?

"Yes?"

"I love hearing that word on your lips, baby cakes."

Her toes curled.

"Where you at?" he asked.

"The ferry. I was in line. I got out."

He stayed quiet so long she thought the call dropped or he hung up.

Did he think she'd hung up on him?

"Luke?"

"Why?" His words were clipped. To her horror, tears welled and her throat choked up. She didn't cry. She reached in her purse for a tissue but came up empty. "Don't cry, baby."

"I'm not."

She spun around and into a warm, hard body.

Luke.

"You're a shit liar."

He took firm hold of her, and she sagged against him, catching stares from people lining up for the next ferry.

"Did you eat?"

She shook her head.

Anchoring her to his side, he walked her back toward the hotel.

⍨⍩⍨

Liz looked out her window at the ominous sky and then read through the press release she was working on one more time before she sent it to her boss for his final approval.

It was four o'clock and, as she scrolled through her inbox, the sky grew darker and darker.

Robert, her boss, came out of his office. "If I read one more thing, my head will explode. Go home before the torrential rain starts."

She smiled and clicked her files closed. "Thanks."

"Where is that, by the way? Home, I mean." He glanced at the three bouquets of red roses on her desk and shrugged. "We used to follow each other home, is all," he said.

Robert was her father's age, married to Cathy for over thirty years, and was a tad over protective.

It was her turn to shrug. "At his place, mostly."

"The guy who came looking for you?"

She grabbed her purse. "Yeah."

"And the sheriff's department approves?"

She smiled. "See you, boss."

She drove half the way to Luke's place and glanced at a billboard for a new health clinic with a picture of a woman with a baby.

Holy hell.

She screeched to a stop at a yellow light.

Her pills. She didn't have her pills. She had them in her rucksack on Mackinaw Island two weeks ago but she hadn't unpacked them and forgot to replace them.

Her stomach rolled.

She hadn't taken a pill for two effing weeks. Luke had kept her so busy in the mornings, when she normally took it, that she didn't even think of it until now.

And he hadn't used protection.

How could she be so stupid?

She gripped her steering wheel and turned her car around. She needed to be in her own space. She needed to buy a pregnancy test.

It took months, sometimes years to get pregnant once you stopped the pill, didn't it?

What if she was pregnant? Had she harmed the baby taking the pills so close to conception? She pulled into a drugstore parking lot, did a search on her cell phone, and scrolled through the answers.

No, it didn't, was the general consensus. Her hand went to her stomach. She grabbed her umbrella and ran into the store.

The cashier was ringing her up when her father walked in.

Shit.

He saw her and smiled. "Hey, sugar." He stepped toward her and his eyes fell on the test just seconds before the cashier slipped it into a bag.

"Elizabeth Ann?"

"It's for a friend." She snatched up the bag and hugged him. "Going to go before it rains."

He kissed her on the forehead. "You're a shit liar, Lizzie."

Running to her car, she got inside just as huge drops of rain pelted the windshield. She drove to her apartment, ignoring texts and then rejecting a call from Luke that synced through her car's sound system. She unlocked her door, found a plastic cup to pee in, dropped the stick, and held her breath.

It was positive.

Her cell phone pinged twice with texts from Luke and her mother.

Perfect.

Call me, Elizabeth from her mother and *Where u at!!!!!* from Luke.

She texted her mother she'd call her tomorrow and texted Luke she was at her place.

I'm almost home. U should have said. U want food? He texted back.

Her stomach growled.

No, don't come.

Y

Headache. Cramps.

He didn't answer. The wind picked up, driving sheets of rain into her windows.

A baby, they'd made a baby. She sat on her couch and hugged her knees. She'd made a baby with the man she loved, and who she demanded divorce her, although the subject hadn't come up in the last two weeks. Neither had love.

She put her cheek on the cushion and let her tears fall.

దిపిప

Luke skidded to a stop at a red light and looked at his phone.

Cramps his ass. Something was up with his wife.

His wife—it was the only way he thought of her. But he hadn't told her he loved her when she was awake to hear it, and he'd stolen her pills.

He'd been desperate that morning when he woke up and she had left. He'd never found the right time or way to give them back, mostly because he simply wanted to make her pregnant, repeatedly, and bind her to him, forever.

But he'd taken the choice away from her.

A horn blared behind him.

Shit. How long had the light been green? He took off as a police squad car with flashing lights pulled up behind him. He pulled over, kept his hands on the steering wheel, and, resisting the urge to reach for his wallet, rolled down the window.

A gust of wind blew the rain inside. He made solid eye contact with the officer who looked pissed and familiar.

It was Liz' brother, Ron, or Ray?

"Get out of the car."

Luke opened his mouth then shut it. Stepping out of the car, he was soaked to his skin in seconds. Liz's brother, who was wearing a rain slicker, smirked.

"Walk in a straight line."

Sloshing through puddles, Luke did it then touched his finger to his nose. Ron or Ray held up a gray box. "This is a Breathalyzer. Would you blow into it, sir?"

Luke could barely see for the water pelting his face. Liz's brother chuckled. He was enjoying it.

"Sure, sir."

The cop barely glanced at the results. "Wait here," he

said, meaning in the rain. He took his time in the squad car while sheets of water dropped from the sky. He stepped back out.

"Don't you need my license and registration?"

"You're kidding, right? We know everything about you. But you need to know this. She fought that piece of shit off and got away from him the way our dad taught her. But she was never the same sweet girl. We want her back."

"We saw the fucker a mile from where I grew up, after the Yankees game. I damned near killed him. She pulled her gun." Luke winced at the memory of her sweet, beautiful face when she saw Rocher. "I couldn't let her. Nothing, no one touches her but me."

Thunder cracked. "Just like the movies." Ron laughed and shook his slicker out. "Get out of the rain." He turned toward the squad car.

Luke pulled out a sweat towel from the bag of baseball stuff he'd left in his back seat to sit on.

"Hey," Liz's brother yelled. "She stopped at the drug store. She had a pregnancy test. And she's a shit liar."

❧❧❧

She sat on her couch, watching the lightning show outside. The texts had stopped. She was feeling both relieved, and sad that he'd given up, when someone pounded on her door.

"Let me in, darling wife." He was dripping wet and holding pizza. "The pizza's dry," he said.

She stood aside to let him in. He set the pizza on the coffee table then hauled her into his arms and kissed her as if he was starved for the taste of her, soaking her clothes with the summer rain. He let her go and peeled off her wet clothes, then his.

"How did you get so wet?"

"It's raining," he deadpanned.

She picked up their wet clothes and hung them over her kitchen chairs. "Most people have the sense to come in out of it."

"Brother dear had other ideas."

Shit. Her dad moved fast. Damn cell phones. But he didn't know the results. She had to destroy the evidence. She moved toward her bathroom.

Luke blocked her path. "Trying to get away from me, babe?"

She moved past him. "Got to pee."

He sprinted past her. "Me, first."

Fuck, fuck, fuck. She sank down on her couch.

Any hope she harbored that he didn't see the test she'd stupidly left there died when he howled for joy.

She covered her face and let her tears fall.

"Hey?" He sat, pulled her onto his lap, and rocked her like a baby. "Shhhh, baby, it's okay."

"I can't be a mother. I'm too messed up. I wanted to shoot you, and I would have killed Evan."

He cupped her face in his hands then wiped away her tears with a napkin. Her stomach growled. Keeping her in his lap, he reached forward, took out a slice of pizza, then held it to her lips.

"Eat."

She took one bite, then another and was down to the crust when he took it away.

"Garlic," he said. "Better?"

She nodded.

"Now we talk. I stole your pills. I guess you figured that out. Desperate times. You gave me that night I wanted, a taste of paradise. Then you rounded for home, away from me, and this. Do you still want to shoot me?"

He looked like he was trying not to laugh.

Anger bubbled up. She squirmed away from him. "Right now, yes."

He pulled her back onto his lap and pressed his face to her chest. "The rest of the time?"

"No."

"Listen, baby, I have killed people in Afghanistan and I saw Smitty after..." His voice trailed off. "I was messed up. I wanted to blame somebody, and I latched on to Amy. And Gray was so crazy in love with her—even though he blamed her, because of Smitty's lies. I knew that he was torn. He would have married her the first time if it wasn't for me. I know that."

She cradled his head in her arms, wanting to comfort him and take his pain away.

"You were my warrior princess, protecting and avenging someone you loved. And you could have killed that piece of shit who assaulted you. But you didn't. He hurt you, and he was still hurting you, and all I could think of was I had to stop him hurting you any further."

It was her turn to say "Shhh." She unhooked her bra, and her breasts, which ached for his touch, sprang free.

"Do you think I'll be a bad father?" He fit her breasts in the palm of his hands. "I have killed people, and my dad wasn't around when I was growing up. I don't know how—"

The fierce warrior instinct he'd described surged to life. She gripped his head so she could look at him. "I've seen you with the twins. You're wonderful. You'll be the best dad."

He played with her nipples, sucking first one, then the other, and slipped his hand under her panties.

"I want you to have a wedding with our families and friends." He let go of her and slid her off of him. He picked up his pants, rummaged in the pocket, pulled out a small black box and dropped to his knees.

"Marry me, baby, for real. I dare you."

She stared at her bare breasts and his dripping wet hair and started to giggle.

The light left his eyes, and she took hold of his face. "Yes, yes. I dare you to marry me in front of Patty and my gun-toting family, but you could have asked me when you weren't soggy and my boobs weren't flapping in the breeze."

He growled. "These luscious breasts do not flap." He slid the emerald cut diamond ring on her finger. It fit.

"How did you know what size?"

He slid next to her and took her in his arms. "We fit. I always knew. Even when you wanted to shoot me. I'm hungry," he said as he laid her back.

Expecting him to take a slice of pizza, she gasped when he lowered his mouth to her navel, then lower, pulling down her pants and lapping her sex until she saw stars.

Chapter 7

Her mother squeezed her hand. Liz was in her old bedroom, watching out the window as wedding guests took their seats on folding chairs overlooking Lake Michigan. Her simple white tulle gown didn't quite hide her baby bump.

"Do you need a salt cracker?" her mom asked. "You should keep something in your stomach."

"I'm good, Mom."

Karen patted her cheek. "You are. He settles you." Her mother blinked back tears. "We have our Lizzie back."

Remembering the mouthy eighteen-year-old she'd

been, she winced. "A new improved version, I hope?"

Karen kissed her cheek then wiped away the lipstick imprint. "Always, precious."

Her father, looking handsome and fit in his tuxedo, put his arm around his wife. "You're on, gorgeous."

Karen smoothed her lacy pink cocktail-style mother-of-the-bride dress over her slim curves. Dan winked at his wife and swatted her bottom as she left them. "How you feeling, precious?"

She dabbed at her eyes, willing herself not to cry. "Okay until you both call me precious."

"You are so precious to us. We wanted a girl so much then you came." Her father's voice cracked. "You know I'd have to mess him up if you weren't already married." He looked away and cleared his throat. "I saw Pete downstairs, the guy who owns the bar. He and his wife came with Patty. He told me what went down that night. He put his liquor license on the line for your soon-to-be, or already husband. He said Luke would have killed that piece of shit with his bare hands."

She couldn't form words past the lump in her throat so she nodded.

"He's a good man. Let's get you married to him—again."

Her father took her arm and they walked across the yard where she played catch with her brothers and the trees just kissed in gold and russet, to the canopy where

Luke stood with Gray, Amy, and Father Fred, the priest who baptized Jack and Jordan.

Luke opted for a black tux tailored to his broad shoulders and slim hips. He'd tamed his wavy hair back away from his face but she missed the lock that usually strayed there.

The priest spoke briefly about canonical law and how doctrine allowed the rite for celebrating marriage outside of Mass, meaning their civil ceremony, then blessed their union.

Luke walked her down the yard before he took her into his arms and claimed her mouth. Their guests, the flowers, and the flute music faded to nothing as his kiss consumed her. Would it always be like this?

Luke insisted they take a honeymoon and she insisted on Mackinaw Island. She loved autumn in Michigan. He held her on the ferry ride, refused to let her carry anything, and held her hand in a death grip on the gang plank.

He let the bellhop take their bags and kept his hands on her disappearing waist as they made their way to the Vanderbilt Suite.

She had only seen photos of the room. A curtained canopy hung over the dark wood bed frame. A purple settee should have clashed with the deep green carpet but the ivory floral bedspread and matching upholstery on the chair and muted green walls made it work.

She tried to stifle a yawn. She felt sleepy all the time. He noticed and pressed her onto the bed.

"Naptime." He settled next to her and undid the buttons on the white dress shirt he wore so she could rest her cheek on his chest, her favorite way to sleep. The last thing she remembered before she drifted off were his hands in her hair.

�''⋄''⋄

She opened her eyes when he set a tray of food on the night stand.

"I thought you'd be hungry," he said.

She drank in his bare chest and jeans that hung low on his lean hips. "I'd rather have you," she said.

He smiled and cupped her face.

"And you shall, sweet wife. But first you eat."

She murmured in protest as her stomach growled. "Shit," she said.

He raised his eyebrows. "Penalty," he said.

They'd discussed this before and shit and hell weren't technically on the list, but she wanted to taste him. He sat next to her and claimed her mouth in a too-brief kiss then fed her bites of chicken, bread dipped in chickpea sauce, and chunks of the fresh pineapple he'd specially ordered that she craved.

Feeling stuffed, she waved him away and went into the plush bathroom to brush her teeth and her hair. She took off her jeans and blouse. She would need maternity pants soon.

Would he still want her?

He came in and stood behind her as she faced the mirror. He caressed the slight swell of her stomach.

"Yes. I can't wait."

Damn. She had voiced her thought out loud.

"The sight of our baby inside you and knowing I put it there…" He trailed off, pressed his face into her neck, and his erection into her backside.

"We never talked about how many we want," he said.

"Two for sure. Then we'll see. Amy and Gray have their hands full with the twins."

"Two at once is different." His head shot up. "Are you, do you think?"

She giggled. "Too soon to tell but Amy popped out right away." She caressed his cheek and smiled at him in the mirror. "I hope he looks like you."

"He?" He nuzzled her neck. "I want our little princess to have chocolate brown eyes with fire in them like her gorgeous mom."

"As long as she can hit a line drive like her gorgeous dad."

His hands moved to the front catch of her blue lacy bra. "Guys are not gorgeous." Her breasts sprang free. He grinned. "I like you in lace but I like you this way best." He palmed her breasts then pinched both nipples. She moaned. He bit down on the tendon between her neck and shoulder. "What do you want, Mrs. Reddington?"

"You."

He slipped his finger inside her blue lacy thong. "Did I say I like these?"

His thumb expertly stroked her sensitive bundle of nerves and she went off like a bottle rocket.

He scooped her up in his arms and carried her to the bed, settling her on her back with her head on the pillows. He stripped out of his jeans and moved the plates of food off the bed. She ogled his washboard abs and runner's butt. How did she get so lucky?

"I'm the lucky one, baby."

Crap. She'd spoken out loud again. She had to stop doing that. She clamped her hand over her mouth.

"Don't. I need all the help you can give me so I can make you as deliriously happy as you make me."

He rose above her and nudged her legs apart.

He had to know how happy she was and how much she loved him, didn't he? Had she ever given him those words? Was that why he hadn't actually ever told her he loved her?

"I love you, Luke, so much."

He shut his eyes. He opened them and they blazed blue like flame. "Say it again."

His erection nudged against her slit. He picked up her left hand and pressed kisses into her palm and the last little wall encasing her heart crumbled.

"I love you, I love you, I love you," she said.

"I love you more than life." He trailed kisses down her throat. "I was afraid to say it out loud until you did." He thrust into her, hitting her sweet spot. She dug her nails into his back, marking him. He pulled out of her. "Say it again."

"I love you."

He eased inside her inch by inch, his cock dragging across her sensitive nerves.

"When?" he said. Sweat dripped off his forehead.

"What?"

"When did you first know?"

She smiled. "That you did it for me?" She kissed him and sucked on his tongue. He surged hard inside her. She pulled her mouth away. "When you dragged me out of that bar in Vegas all caveman like when that guy grabbed my ass and I saw how fine your ass looked when you led me out of there."

He moved his hips, hitting her sweet spot and she came hard, screaming his name. His eyes never left her face.

"So you dared me to marry you, thinking I would run away from you," he said.

Panting hard, she tried to gather her thoughts. "You're fucking the truth out of me," she said.

His eyes narrowed. "Penalty, and yes." He pounded into her then stopped short as she teetered on the brink, again. "Answer me."

She nodded. "Yes, after Evan—"

He clamped his hand over her mouth. "Don't say his name, baby. I can't stand it. The light leaves your eyes when you do. I get it. I'll never hurt you. And I'll never let anyone else hurt you either. You know that, right?"

She nodded and he pounded into her. She shut her eyes as her climax washed through her and he emptied himself inside her then collapsed on top of her.

He eased out of her and held her in his arms as the room grew darker and darker.

"You're mine, Liz."

"I know, I've always known. I was scared to trust it. I'm not now."

She traced lazy circles along his chest and down his stomach and felt his erection press into her side.

"Show me, baby. I dare you."

So she did.

THE END

About the Author

Tara Eldana, pen name, is an award-winning staff writer for a weekly community newspaper chain in metro Detroit. She became hooked on romance fiction when her eleventh grade English teacher rejected the book report she wrote, saying the book was much too easy for her, and insisted she read and report on Daphne du Maurier's *Rebecca*. She had read Margaret Mitchell's *Gone With the Wind* that previous summer.

Eldana took a long road through J-school, graduating from Oakland University in Rochester, Michigan in '95, just shy of 20 years after she finished high school, raising a couple kids, working part-time, and doing her homework while her husband and kids watched TV. Still she found time to read what her kids called her "mush books."

She loves the romance genre and loves letting her characters take control of their stories. Eldana is a member of the Greater Detroit Romance Writers of America.